TRACTOR MAC
BUILDS A BARN

Written and illustrated by
BILLY STEERS

FARRAR STRAUS GIROUX • NEW YORK

AROUND AND AROUND turned Tractor Mac's big tires. Rolling through the fields was what Tractor Mac liked best.

He loved to chat with his friends as he moved around the farm carrying out his chores. Through the farmyard, down the dirt lanes, across the fields—there were always new things to see and do.

"You don't ever stop moving, do you,
Tractor Mac?" clucked Carla the chicken.
"I would never get any work done if
I weren't moving," laughed Tractor Mac.
"I have wheels! I've got to use them!"
"A rolling tractor gathers no rust!"
added Goat Walter.

CHUG CHUGGA POPPA! You could hear Mac rumble across the fields and woodlots from dawn until dusk.

"You never sit still long enough for us to chat," said Lucy, his tractor friend from next door.

Mac blushed a deeper shade of red. "Sorry, Lucy," he said with a smile. "I have wheels! I have to use them!"

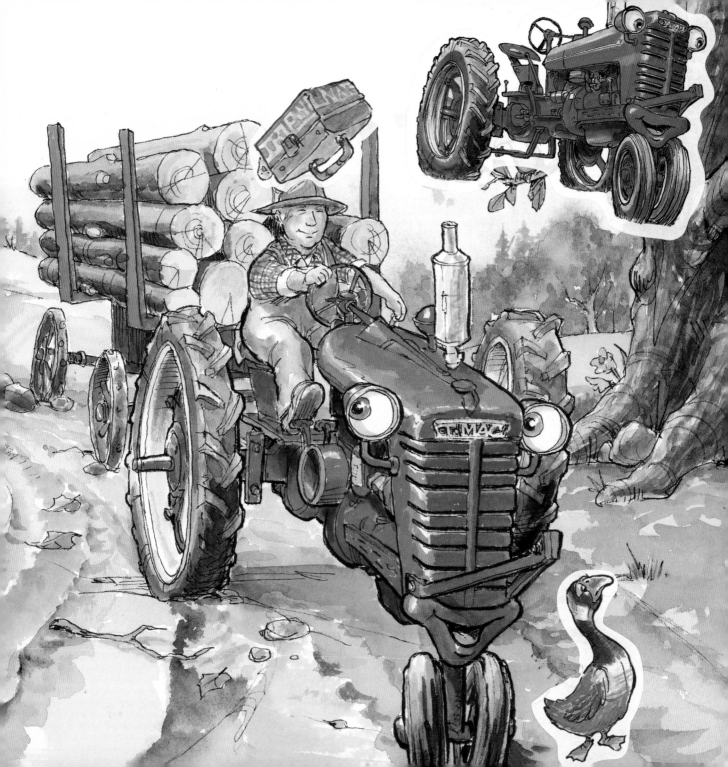

As he backed Tractor Mac into the shed that night, Farmer Bill said, "This old shed is getting to be a tight fit. We are going to need more room. Tomorrow, Mac, we start a *different* type of work."

Early the next morning, Farmer Bill parked Mac next to the old shed. With a leather belt he connected Mac to a big machine.

Mac hoped he would not be sitting still for too long. He wanted to work in the fields.

All day, Mac ran the sawmill. It was noisy and dirty work. Dust kept flying into his air cleaner.

The leather belt spun. **Flip, Flap, Fwip!** Day after day, Mac just sat and ran his power wheel. Farmer Bill even removed one of his big tires to fix a leak. Boy, did Mac feel silly!

"I love the smell of woodchips, don't you?" said Carla, trying to cheer him up.

Lucy was helping Sibley the horse haul
more wood for Mac to cut and split.

"Won't you stay and chat?" asked Mac.

"Sorry," said Lucy with a smile. "*I've* got
wheels! I have to use them!"

Mac felt so out of place. Everybody on the farm was moving around except for him! How was he supposed to get any work done just sitting there getting covered with dust? Still, Mac did his best to keep his belt running steady and smooth.

"Farmer Bill's wife could plant flowers around you!" laughed Pete and Paul the pigs.

One day, Farmer Bill came and finally took off the big belt. Mac's tire had been fixed and was put back on his axle.

"It's time for you to see what you've been doing these past few weeks," said Sibley to his friend.

Mac turned the corner and saw his neighbors had all gathered. It seemed as if half the town was there! Lucy was there, too!

It was a barn raising! Axes and hammers flew. By late morning, Tractor Mac and Lucy had helped raise the first wall. The people and animals all cheered.

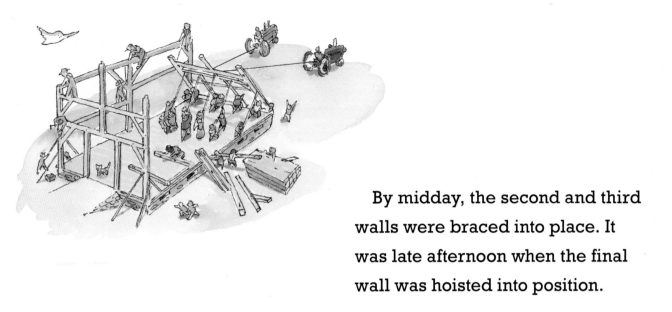

By midday, the second and third walls were braced into place. It was late afternoon when the final wall was hoisted into position.

The rafters were pegged into place, and a small evergreen was placed on the top for good luck.

"It's amazing," said Lucy. "You not only raised this barn—you made it, too! Plank, board, and beam!"

"Stupendous!" squealed Pete the pig. "I thought tractors were only good for field work. I didn't know they could build barns, too!"

"Neither did I," laughed Tractor Mac.

"Neither did I!"